Feliz cumpleaños, querido dragón

Happy Birthday, Dear Dragon

por/by Margaret Hillert

Ilustrado por/Illustrated by Jack Pullan

NORWOOD HOUSE PRESS

Querido padre o tutor: Es posible que los libros de esta serie para lectores principiantes les resulten familiares, ya que las versiones originales de los mismos podrían haber formado parte de sus primeras lecturas. Estos textos, cuidadosamente escritos, incluyen palabras de uso frecuente que le proveen al niño la oportunidad de familiarizarse con las más comúnmente usadas en el lenguaje escrito. Estas nuevas versiones han sido actualizadas y las encantadoras ilustraciones son sumamente atractivas para una nueva generación de pequeños lectores.

Primero, léale el cuento al niño, después permita que él lea las palabras con las que esté familiarizado, y pronto podrá leer solito todo el cuento. En cada paso, elogie el esfuerzo del niño para que desarrolle confianza como lector independiente. Hable sobre las ilustraciones y anime al niño a relacionar el cuento con su propia vida.

Al final del cuento, encontrará actividades relacionadas con la lectura que ayudarán a su niño a practicar y fortalecer sus habilidades como lector. Estas actividades, junto con las preguntas de comprensión, se adhieren a los estándares actuales, de manera que la lectura en casa apoyará directamente los objetivos de instrucción en el salón de clase.

Sobre todo, la parte más importante de toda la experiencia de la lectura es ¡divertirse y disfrutarla!

Dear Caregiver: The books in this Beginning-to-Read collection may look somewhat familiar in that the original versions could have been a part of your own early reading experiences. These carefully written texts feature common sight words to provide your child multiple exposures to the words appearing most frequently in written text. These new versions have been updated and the engaging illustrations are highly appealing to a contemporary audience of young readers.

Begin by reading the story to your child, followed by letting him or her read familiar words and soon your child will be able to read the story independently. At each step of the way, be sure to praise your reader's efforts to build his or her confidence as an independent reader. Discuss the pictures and encourage your child to make connections between the story and his or her own life.

At the end of the story, you will find reading activities that will help your child practice and strengthen beginning reading skills. These activities, along with the comprehension questions are aligned to current standards, so reading efforts at home will directly support the instructional goals in the classroom.

Above all, the most important part of the reading experience is to have fun and enjoy it!

Shannon Cannon

Shannon Cannon, Ph.D., Consultora de lectoescritura / Literacy Consultant

Norwood House Press • www.norwoodhousepress.com
Beginning-to-Read ™ is a registered trademark of Norwood House Press.
Illustration and cover design copyright ©2018 by Norwood House Press. All Rights Reserved.

Authorized Bilingual adaptation from the U.S. English language edition, entitled Happy Birthday, Dear Dragon by Margaret Hillert. Copyright © 2017 Margaret Hillert. Bilingual adaptation Copyright © 2018 Margaret Hillert. Translated and adapted with permission. All rights reserved. Pearson and Feliz cumpleaños, querido dragón are trademarks, in the US and/or other countries, of Pearson Education, Inc. or its affiliates. This publication is protected by copyright, and prior permission to re-use in any way in any format is required by both Norwood House Press and Pearson Education. This book is authorized in the United States for use in schools and public libraries.

LIBRARY OF CONGRESS CATALOGING-IN-PUBLICATION DATA
Names: Hillert, Margaret, author. | Pullan, Jack, illustrator. | Del Risco,
    Eida, translator.
Title: ¡Feliz cumpleaños, Querido Dragón! : Happy birthday, Dear Dragon / por
    Margaret Hillert ; ilustrado por Jack Pullan ; traducido por Eida Del Risco.
Other titles: Happy birthday, Dear Dragon
Description: Chicago, IL : Norwood House Press, [2017] | Series: A
    beginning-to-read book | Summary: "A young boy celebrates his birthday and
    receives a pet dragon as a gift. The two play and become the best of
    friends. Spanish/English edition includes reading activities"-- Provided by publisher.
Identifiers: LCCN 2016053217 (print) | LCCN 2017014203 (ebook) | ISBN
    9781684040292 (eBook) | ISBN 9781599538303 (library edition : alk. paper)
Subjects: | CYAC: Birthdays--Fiction. | Dragons--Fiction. | Spanish language
    materials--Bilingual.
Classification: LCC PZ73 (ebook) | LCC PZ73 .H5572064 2017 (print) | DDC
    [E]--dc23
LC record available at https://lccn.loc.gov/2016053217

Hardcover ISBN: 978-1-59953-830-3   Paperback ISBN: 978-1-68404-016-2

302N—072017
Manufactured in the United States of America in North Mankato, Minnesota.

Luce bien, mamá.
Qué grande.
Oh, qué divertido.

This looks good, Mother.
What a big one.
Oh, this is fun.

Aquí hay algo.
¿Qué es?
No puedo adivinar.

Here is something.
What is it?
I can not guess.

Oh, mira aquí.
¡Mira esto
y esto
y esto!

Oh, look here.
Look at this
—and this
—and this!

5

Y aquí hay algo que puede saltar.

And here is something that can jump up.

Ahora ven conmigo.
Quiero darte algo.
¡Corre, corre, corre!

Now come with me.
I want to get you something.
Run, run run!

Vamos a entrar aquí.
Es aquí. Es aquí.
Vamos a mirar los perros.

Here we go.
In here. In here.
We will look at dogs.

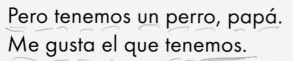

Pero tenemos un perro, papá.
Me gusta el que tenemos.

But we have a dog, Father.
I like the one we have.

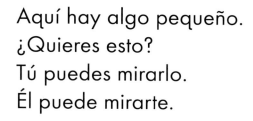

Aquí hay algo pequeño.
¿Quieres esto?
Tú puedes mirarlo.
Él puede mirarte.

Here is something little.
Do you want this?
You can look at it.
It can look at you.

No, no lo quiero.
¿Qué puede hacer?
No puede jugar conmigo.

No, I do not want it.
What can it do?
It can not play with me.

Mira aquí abajo.
Puedes tener este.
¿Te gusta?
Míralo saltar.

Look down here.
You can have this one.
Do you like it?
See it jump.

¡ADOPTA UNA MASCOTA!
ADOPT A PET!

Me gusta ese pequeño.
Pero no es lo que quiero.
Ven aquí.
Ven aquí.

I like that little one.
But it is not what I want.
Come here.
Come here.

Aquí está lo que quiero.
Anda, ¿me lo compras?
Me gusta.
Me gusta.
Me gusta.

Here is what I want.
Oh, will you get it for me?
I like it.
I like it.
I like it!

Ven conmigo.
Ven a mi casa.
Me caes bien.
Podemos divertirnos.

Come with me.
Come to my house.
I like you.
We can have fun.

COMIDA DE
DRAGÓN
DRAGON
FOOD

Mira, mamá.
Mira lo que tengo.
Puede jugar conmigo.

Look, Mother.
See what I have.
It can play with me.

Ya veo.
Ya veo.
Es gracioso.
Le vamos a buscar algo.

I see.
I see.
It is funny.
We will find something for it.

Quiero dar un paseo.
Voy a subirme.
Ayúdame.
Ayúdame.

I want to go for a ride.
I will get in.
Help me.
Help me.

Allá vamos.
¡Corre, corre, corre!
¡Qué divertido!
¡Qué divertido!

Here we go.
Run, run, run!
What fun!
What fun!

¿Harás algo por mí?
¿Me ayudarás con esto?

Will you do something for me?
Will you help me with this?

Toma uno.
Toma dos.
Toma tres.
Eres una gran ayuda.

Have one.
Have two.
Have three.
You are a big help.

Caramba.
Caramba.
Mira lo que puedes hacer.
¡Esto me gusta!

Oh, my.
Oh, my.
Look what you can do.
I like this!

Tú estás conmigo.
Y yo estoy contigo.

Here you are with me.
And here I am with you.

Ay, qué cumpleaños tan feliz,
querido dragón.

Oh, what a happy birthday,
Dear Dragon.

29

READING REINFORCEMENT

The following activities support the findings of the National Reading Panel that determined the most effective components for reading instruction are: Phonemic Awareness, Phonics, Vocabulary, Fluency, and Text Comprehension.

Phonemic Awareness: The /d/ sound

Sound Substitution: Say the words on the left to your child. Ask your child to repeat the word, changing the first sound to /**d**/:

pot - /d/ = dot   junk - /d/ = dunk   keep - /d/ = deep
bent - /d/ = dent   fish - /d/ = dish   near - /d/ = dear
time - /d/ = dime   kid - /d/ = did   rip - /d/ = dip

Phonics: The letter Dd

1. Demonstrate how to form the letters **D** and **d** for your child.

2. Have your child practice writing **D** and **d** at least three times each.

3. Ask your child to point to the words in the book that start with the letter **d.**

4. Write down the following words and ask your child to circle the letter **d** in each word:

do	dragon	dog	dear	day
food	wood	dad	den	hand
riddle	sad	doll	puddle	dig

Vocabulary: Naming Objects

1. Ask your child to tell you different words he or she thinks of that go with "birthday". Write the words on sticky notes and have the child place them next to any objects he or she has named that are in the story.

2. Ask your child to tell a story using all of the words he or she has come up with that relate to birthday.

Fluency: Echo Reading

1. Reread the story to your child at least two more times while your child tracks the print by running a finger under the words as they are read. Ask your child to read the words he or she knows with you.

2. Reread the story, stopping after each sentence or page to allow your child to read (echo) what you have read. Repeat echo reading and let your child take the lead.

Text Comprehension: Discussion Time

1. Ask your child to retell the sequence of events in the story.

2. To check comprehension, ask your child the following questions:

   • Why didn't the boy want the dog for his birthday?
   • Why didn't the boy want the fish for his birthday?
   • Which parts of this story could really happen?
   • Which parts of this story couldn't really happen?
   • Which pet would you choose? Why?

ACERCA DE LA AUTORA Margaret Hillert ha ayudado a millones de niños de todo el mundo a aprender a leer independientemente. Fue maestra de primer grado por 34 años y durante esa época empezó a escribir libros con los que sus estudiantes pudieran ganar confianza en la lectura y pudieran, al mismo tiempo, disfrutarla. Ha escrito más de 100 libros para niños que comienzan a leer. De niña, disfrutaba escribiendo poesía y, de adulta, continuó su escritura poética tanto para niños como para adultos.

Photograph by Glenna Washburn

ABOUT THE AUTHOR Margaret Hillert has helped millions of children all over the world learn to read independently. She was a first grade teacher for 34 years and during that time started writing books that her students could both gain confidence in reading and enjoy. She wrote well over 100 books for children just learning to read. As a child, she enjoyed writing poetry and continued her poetic writings as an adult for both children and adults.

ACERCA DEL ILUSTRADOR Jack Pullan, ilustrador talentoso y creativo, es graduado de William Jewell College. También ha estudiado informalmente en la Universidad de Oxford y en el Instituto de Arte de Kansas City. Sus mentores han sido los renombrados acuarelistas Jim Hamil y Bill Amend. La obra de Jack ha adornado las páginas de numerosos y placenteros libros para niños, diversos materiales educativos y tiras cómicas, así como también muchas tarjetas de felicitación. Jack reside actualmente en Kansas.

ABOUT THE ILLUSTRATOR A talented and creative illustrator, Jack Pullan, is a graduate of William Jewell College. He has also studied informally at Oxford University and the Kansas City Art Institute. He was mentored by the renowned watercolor artists, Jim Hamil and Bill Amend. Jack's work has graced the pages of many enjoyable children's books, various educational materials, cartoon strips, as well as many greeting cards. Jack currently resides in Kansas.